THE SAME BUT DIFFERENT

Library of Congress number: 89-3833

Library of Congress Cataloging in Publication Data

Goldish, Meish.
  The same but different/Meish Goldish; Illustrated by Monica Santa Loomis.

  (Real readers)
  Summary: Rhyming text and illustrations follow the adventures of the Little family when
they decide to travel and see new places.
  [1. Voyages and travels — Fiction. 2. Stories in rhyme.] I. Loomis, Monica Santa, ill. II.
Title. III. Series.
PZ8.3.G5695Sam 1989   [E] — dc19   89-3833
ISBN: 0-8172-3528-0

1 2 3 4 5 6 7 8 9 0   93 92 91 90 89

The SAME but DIFFERENT

by Meish Goldish
illustrated by
Monica Santa Loomis

Raintree Publishers
Milwaukee

Mr. Little lived in Glome,
In a cozy little home.
He had lived there all his life
With his children and his wife.

Every day when day began,
Mr. Little ate and ran,
Running to his job in town,
Working till the sun went down.

Every night he came back home,
Walking in the streets of Glome.
Mr. Little, at day's end,
Smiled and waved to every friend.

Week by week, he did the same.
To his job he went and came.

Off to work, he walked to town,
Working till the sun went down.
Every night he came back home,
Never, ever leaving Glome.

One day, Mr. Little said,
"What a dull life I have led!
I only know my job and home,
I've never been outside of Glome.
Me, oh, my, what I would give
To see how other people live!"

Mr. Little told his wife,
"We have only seen this life.
Let us go to some place new
And see the different things they do."

Mrs. Little said, "Okay.
Trains take people far away.
There's a station in this town.
We can go there and sit down.
That's the thing that we must do
If we're going somewhere new."

All the Littles walked through town.
In the station, they sat down.
No train came while they sat there,
But the Littles didn't care.

They never took a trip before,
So they sat still by the door.

They thought you go from place to place
Just by sitting in your space!
You see, the Littles didn't know
You must be on the train to go!

When they thought the trip was done,
Mr. Little said, "What fun!
Taking trips is such a breeze!
Sit and go to where you please!

Now I think we'll walk outside
After such a long, long ride.
"In this new town, we will hike.
We will learn what it is like."

14

All the Littles walked the street,
Looking for a place to eat.
Soon they saw a big food store,
One they thought they'd seen before.

Mrs. Little said, "Back home
There's a store like this in Glome!
The store back home from where we came
And this new store look <u>just</u> <u>the</u> <u>same</u>!"

All the Littles walked for miles.
Greeting people with big smiles.
Funny, how each different face
Seemed like one they'd seen someplace.

Mr. Little said, "Back home
People look like this in Glome!
The people back from where we came
And people here look just the same!"

All the Littles walked till dark.
Then they saw a pretty park.
Mrs. Little looked once more.
It looked like one she'd seen before.

Mrs. Little said, "Back home
There's a park like this in Glome!
The park back home from where we came
And this new park look <u>just</u> <u>the</u> <u>same</u>!"

20

Soon they saw on one fine street
A house so cozy and so sweet,
Mr. Little had to groan,
"This looks like the house <u>we</u> own!

Our own house from where we came
And this new house look <u>just</u> <u>the</u> <u>same</u>!"
How I wish we were in Glome.
Let us hurry and go home."

All the Littles walked through town.
In the station, they sat down.
In the station, they did stay,
Thinking they were on the way.

They thought you go from place to place
Just by sitting in your space.
You see, the Littles didn't know
You must be <u>on</u> the train to go!

24

When they thought the trip was done,
Mr. Little said, "What fun!
Taking trips is such a breeze!
Sit and go to where you please!"

All the Littles went outside
Thinking they had had a ride.
Then they walked home in the street,
Waving to each friend they'd meet.

Their friends all smiled and said, "Hello!
Tell us all, where did you go?
Did you travel up and down?
Did you see a different town?

"Tell us of the time you spent
In the places where you went.
Tell us of the news you bring,
Tell us, tell us everything!"

Mr. Little thought awhile.
On his face, he had a smile.
Then he said, "We learned a lot
Being in a different spot.

"All the stores, it seems most clear,
Are different, but just like ones here!
All the people where you go
Are different, but like ones we know!
Every park, and every home
Is different, but like those in Glome!

"From our trip, we now can claim:
The world is different, but the same!"

Sharing the Joy of Reading

Beginning readers enjoy reading books on their own. Reading a book is a worthwhile activity in and of itself for a young reader. However, a child's reading can be even more rewarding if it is shared. This sharing can enhance your child's appreciation — both of the book and of his or her own abilities.

   Now that your child has read **The Same but Different**, you can help extend your child's reading experience by encouraging him or her to:

• Retell the story or key concepts presented in this story in his or her own words. The retelling can be oral or written.

• Create a picture of a favorite character, event, or concept from this book.

• Express his or her own ideas and feelings about the characters in this book and other things the characters might do.

Here is an activity that you can do together to help extend your child's appreciation of this book: You and your child can talk about the community in which you live. Are there any parks? Where do you shop for food? What does the street you live on look like? When you have finished your discussion, your child might like to draw a picture of your street or some other part of the community.